SUSIE
The Orphan

Home Farm Twins

1 Speckle The Stray
2 Sinbad The Runaway
3 Solo The Homeless
4 Susie The Orphan
5 Spike The Tramp
6 Snip And Snap The Truants
7 Sunny The Hero
8 Socks The Survivor
9 Stevie The Rebel
10 Samson The Giant
11 Sultan The Patient
12 Sorrel The Substitute
13 Skye The Champion
14 Sugar and Spice The Pickpockets
Scruffy The Scamp

Susie

The Orphan

Jenny Oldfield

Illustrated by Kate Aldous

*Hodder
Children's
Books*

a division of Hodder Headline plc

A Catalogue record for this book is available from the British Library

ISBN 0 340 66130 5

Typeset by Avon Dataset Ltd, Bidford-on-Avon, Warks

Printed and bound in Great Britain by
Cox & Wyman Ltd, Reading, Berks

Hodder Children's Books
a division of Hodder Headline plc
338 Euston Road ·
London NW1 3BH

One

'Come by!' The farmer called his dog down Doveton Fell.

'Speckle, come and look at Ben.' Helen sat on a wall with her twin sister, Hannah, and their dad, David Moore. 'Ben's a real champion!'

The sheepdog chased three stray sheep downhill to join the flock. He ran, then crouched low, waiting for the next command.

'Come in!' John Fox called. 'Ben, come in!'

It was the order to move the sheep on. The clever sheepdog drove them through the gate into the field.

'Ben's brilliant.' Hannah felt like clapping. 'He's so clever.'

'And fit.' Helen, too, loved to watch.

'Yes, but sheep are pretty silly,' David Moore pointed out. He thought that rounding them up was simple.

'No, they're not!' The twins jumped off the wall and turned to him.

'Sheep can climb mountains.' Helen stood, hands on hips.

'They can reach places other people can't reach!' added Hannah.

'OK.' David Moore put his hands up in surrender. 'I give in. Sheep are amazing too.' He stood with his camera slung around his neck, grinning at his daughters.

'And lambs. Did you know, they can stand up as soon as they're born?' Hannah had watched some of Mr Fox's sheep give birth at Lakeside Farm in early spring.

'I wish we had lambs at Home Farm,' Helen sighed.

The Moore family had moved from the city into a run-down farm in the Lake District. They weren't farmers, but the twins loved animals. By hook or by crook, they hoped to persuade their mum and dad to fill Home Farm with dogs, cats, chickens, rabbits, goats, ponies . . . and now lambs.

'Uh-oh!' Their dad stuck his fingers in his ears. 'I didn't hear that!' He took photographs for a living. The twins' mum, Mary, ran a small café in nearby Nesfield. They said they didn't have time to look after more animals.

'Lambs are cute.' Hannah opened her big brown eyes and peered up at him from under her thick fringe.

'Lambs are white and fluffy, with little black faces and springy legs,' Helen said.

'Yes, and lambs grow up into great big sheep!' David Moore fiddled with the lens of his camera. 'Come on, I thought you two wanted to help.'

'We do.' Helen pulled off her sweater and tied the sleeves around her waist. 'But it's hot.'

They were helping him to take photographs of Doveton Fell in spring. The fell was covered in yellow, white and pink flowers, the farms were full of black and white calves on wobbly legs, fluffy yellow chickens, and of course, beautiful lambs.

3

'Come on, Speckle,' Hannah sighed.

Their young border collie leapt to his feet. He ran ahead, black coat shining in the sun, speckled legs racing over the rough ground.

'Did you see the lambs?' Helen strode on with Hannah. 'They're growing big and sturdy.'

'Yes, but there are still a few tiny ones.' These were the babies that stuck close to their mothers. Ben had been gentle with them, nudging and taking care not to scare them.

'Dad!' Suddenly Helen caught hold of her sister's arm and turned to catch his attention. Speckle had raised a big bird from its nest among the heather. It was fat and red, with flashes of greeny-blue and black.

Click! The camera caught the grouse as it spread its wings. *Click, click, whir!*

They walked on, higher up the steep hill, leaving Lakeside Farm behind. From way up here they could see the blue lake and Doveton village like a toy town nestling at the water's edge.

'Shh!' It was Hannah's turn to spot a good picture. A rabbit sat sleepily in the sun at the roots of a hawthorn tree. He was brown and soft, with long, twitching ears.

Click! David Moore pointed his camera. The shutter snapped open and closed. The rabbit vanished in an instant.

'Did you get him?' Hannah's eyes shone with excitement.

He nodded. 'Good one.' He hoped to sell these photographs to a wildlife magazine. 'Thanks, girls.' He looked at his watch. 'It's nearly lunchtime, thank heavens.'

But before they cut across the fell to make their way home, Helen and Hannah saw Speckle chase still higher, towards a pointed rock surrounded by loose, flat stones. He ran, nose to the ground, a long way off.

'Speckle, lie down!' Hannah had learned this command from John Fox. It meant 'Stop!'

The young dog heard and reluctantly did as he was told.

'What's up there?' Helen was curious. Speckle didn't usually run so far ahead.

'I don't know. But my stomach knows that it wants its lunch,' David Moore complained.

'Come by!' Hannah's call echoed over the empty hill.

Speckle came as called. But when he reached the twins, he lifted his head and gave a sharp bark. Then he ran two or three steps back up the slope.

'There's something up there.' Helen listened. 'And Speckle wants us to follow him.'

Speckle barked again, took another few steps.

'That'll do, Speckle!' David Moore said briskly, meaning, 'The job's finished. It's time for lunch.'

The dog and the twins all looked at him with pleading eyes. 'Can't we just take a look?' Hannah asked. 'You don't have to come. You could stop here.'

'We'll take the camera, in case it's something interesting.' Helen put an arm around Speckle's neck, telling him to wait.

Happy to have a rest before they went home, their dad handed over the camera and Hannah gave Speckle the order to lead on. They followed as fast as they could, but their legs soon ached and their breath came short. It was a steep hill and the day was hot.

'Did you hear that?' Helen saw Speckle stop in the same spot as before, in the shadow of the pointed rock. There was a tiny, high bleating sound.

Hannah nodded. Already breathless and tired,

they broke into a run. Their feet slid and skidded on the loose rocks. The bleats grew louder as Speckle poked his nose into the shadows.

There, out of sight, deep in the shadow of the rock, lay a fleecy white lamb. Her face and legs were black, her eyes big and shining. Helen raised the camera and took the perfect picture.

'Good boy, Speckle!' Hannah hugged him. She turned to Helen. 'But where's the mother?'

They looked all around; at the high rocks above, down the hill into the valley.

Helen shook her head. 'Not round here.'

'The lamb must be lost. I wonder where she comes from.' Hannah watched as she bleated and struggled to her feet. 'I think she's only a few days old.'

'What shall we do?' Helen knew that tiny lambs ought not to be kept apart from their mothers.

'We can't leave her here.' Down below, their dad lay stretched out on the heather, sunning himself. 'Let's try to find her mother.' Gently Hannah bent forward to lift the lamb in her arms. The little creature bleated again and struggled. 'She's light as a feather.'

Speckle jumped up and sniffed at the lamb, as if he too was worried. He tried to herd Hannah down the hill, rounding her up from behind and waiting for her to carry the lamb down.

'He's telling you where to go,' Helen said. She ran to explain to their dad, who beckoned for Hannah to bring the lost lamb down.

'Let's have a look at this little lady.' He took the trembling white creature into his strong arms. 'There, we'll soon sort you out.'

Helen smiled at Hannah. Their dad was as soft on animals as they were, if only he would admit it. He cuddled the lamb close to his cheek.

'No sign of the mother, eh?' David Moore nodded down the valley towards Lakeside Farm. 'What do you think?'

The twins nodded. 'Let's take her to Mr Fox,' said Helen.

'He'll know what to do,' agreed Hannah.

'The poor little thing probably belongs to him in any case.' He handed her on to an eager Helen. 'It looks like she got left behind by Ben. We'd better get her down there as soon as we can.'

So they set off carefully carrying the lamb in turns, with Speckle running ahead. The white flash at the tip of his tail bobbed clear of the ferns and heather. Soon they came through the field of sheep to John Fox's farmyard.

Ben greeted them with a loud bark and a welcoming wag of his tail.

The old farmer came out of a stone barn, his cap pushed back, his shirt sleeves rolled, his waistcoat hanging open. 'Now then.' He eyed the lamb in Hannah's arms. 'It looks like one you left behind, Ben, old chap.'

The twins thought he sounded worried. There

was a frown on his face as he came to take a closer look.

'We found her by the pointed rock, halfway up the scree.' Helen looked anxiously at him.

'You mean the Needle? She's one of mine, right enough.' He shook his head. 'I've got her twin sister here in the barn.'

Hannah nuzzled against the lamb's soft fleece. The little thing bleated and licked her cheek. Their lost lamb was a twin, then.

'Where's their mother?' Helen too was worried. 'Why is the sister lamb in the barn?'

'That's just it, you see.' Mr Fox shrugged. 'She hasn't got one. The mother died last night.'

The twins stared. A lump came into their throats.

The farmer explained. 'She was a bad doer, as a matter of fact. I mean, she was never very strong. Twins was too much for her, see. I found her on the fell first thing this morning. There was nothing I could do.' He offered to take the lamb from Hannah. 'I found one twin and brought her down. But we missed this one. To tell you the truth, I thought she'd been stolen.'

'Stolen?' Helen echoed.

'Aye, I've lost a few sheep that way these last few weeks. Still, all's well that ends well.' He studied the lost lamb with an expert eye.

'Will she be all right?' Hannah held on tight. The lamb snuggled up warm against her.

'You'll find her a foster-mother, won't you?' David Moore stepped forward, trying to be cheerful. 'Another sheep who can look after her?'

The old man scratched his head. 'I would as a rule, aye . . .'

'But?' Helen guessed that something bad came next.

'But I've already fostered the other twin on my last spare ewe. I don't have any others.' He shrugged. 'This one will have to be bottle-fed.'

'Hand-reared?' Hannah reached out to stroke the orphan's head. 'Poor little thing.'

The lamb gave a tiny bleat. Without a mother or a foster-mother, she was alone in the world.

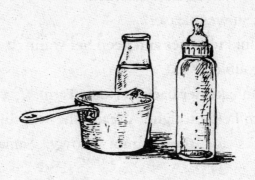

Two

'Yes, and it all takes time,' John Fox sighed. 'I've got sheep to dip, and I begin clipping in a week or two. I've got my hands full.' He went on scratching his head, as if hand-rearing Helen and Hannah's lamb was one job too many.

Hannah held on to the small white orphan, while Helen turned to her dad.

'I'll have to bottle-feed her for twelve weeks before she's ready to go it alone.' The old farmer looked shrewdly at his visitors. 'I don't suppose you two would fancy having a go?'

'Oh!' they gasped.

'Would we!' Hannah breathed.

'Dad, can we, please?'

'We could feed her and keep her warm. It won't be any trouble.'

'We can take her back to Home Farm.'

Hannah held on tight. Already she was thinking up names for their lamb: Snowy, Samantha, Susie . . .

'You're sure you can't find her a new mother?' David Moore ran a hand through his wavy hair. The sun shone bright on Hannah's chestnut brown hair, and on the lamb's white fleece. Another perfect shot for his camera, except that Hannah's face was too serious.

'As sure as eggs is eggs,' John Fox said.

They waited what seemed like ages for their father's answer.

He ummed and aahed. He shrugged. 'Well, what's one animal more or less?' he sighed at last.

Hannah and Helen let out a yell. 'Thanks, Dad!'

John Fox winked. 'Come with me. I'll show you how it's done.' He led them into the warm, dark barn. 'Lie down, Ben,' he said smartly.

'Lie down, Speckle,' Helen ordered.

The two dogs settled outside the door.

Inside the barn were half a dozen sickly lambs and their ewes, bleating feebly. John Fox checked them before he went to the farmhouse kitchen to fetch a kettle filled with warm water. He poured some into a chipped cup. 'Now,' he said, holding up a small bottle which he took from his pocket. 'Brandy! A drop of this will soon get her back on her feet.' He poured a tablespoon of brown liquid into the water. 'Hold her still.'

Hannah felt the lamb wriggle as Mr Fox tilted her head back and gently eased the drink between her lips. When it was all gone, he stood back. 'Righto, let's try her on her feet, shall we?'

Gently Hannah lowered the lamb on to the stone floor. The others kept their fingers crossed.

'Oh!' Hannah gasped. The lamb tottered and fell. But she raised herself and stood on wobbly legs. She flicked her ears, licked her lips.

'Champion,' Mr Fox said with a nod. 'It's warm milk she needs from now on. Diluted cows' milk from a bottle. It's just like feeding a baby, you'll see.'

* * *

'Susie!' Helen helped Hannah decide on a name for the lamb as they walked home from Lakeside Farm later that afternoon. It was her turn to carry the orphan wrapped inside her sweater. A breeze had got up while they were in the barn learning how to feed her, and clouds had covered the sun. 'Don't you think she looks like a Susie?'

Hannah nodded happily. A lamb at Home Farm. True, they would only have Susie with them for a few weeks, until she was ready to go back to Mr Fox's flock. But they would take care of her and bring her up to be strong and healthy, just like her real mother would have done.

'Rain,' their dad muttered, looking up at the dark sky. Quickly he zipped his camera inside its case. 'Here it comes.'

In Doveton the weather could change from fine to wet within minutes. Clouds gathered over the high fell and burst without warning.

'Susie will get wet,' Helen gasped, hurrying on.

'So will I. And I haven't got a woolly coat *and* a sweater to keep me dry!' Their dad was soaked through to the skin by the time they reached their lane.

'It's only an April shower,' Hannah giggled as she held the gate open. Rain dripped from the tip of their dad's nose. They ran for the house across the stone-flagged yard. The rabbits, Sugar and Spice, were snug in their hutch, the hens had scuttled into the barn to keep dry. Wet through, David Moore unlocked the kitchen door and staggered in.

'Fetch a towel!' Helen carried Susie to the warm stove. She began to rub her head and back, working the towel in small, gentle circles until the lamb was dry.

'Let's wrap her up in it,' Hannah suggested. She thought Susie looked cold and miserable.

'And give her a feed.' They'd brought the bottles and rubber teats from Lakeside Farm. Helen stood at the stove heating a pan of milk. She poured it steadily into a bottle, then looked on with a worried frown as Hannah tried to get Susie to drink.

Hannah sat cross-legged on the floor, resting the lamb on her lap. With one arm hooked around her middle, she held the bottle to her lips. Susie turned her head away. Hannah tried again. Once more she eased the teat against her lips. This time, the lamb opened her mouth and began to suck, slowly at first, then strongly gulping it down.

'There!' Helen smiled.

'Don't give her too much,' David Moore warned. His hair was still wringing wet from the rain. 'Remember, John said little and often.' He hovered at a distance with Speckle.

'She's a greedy little thing!' Helen watched the milk disappear.

'She'll burst!' Hannah gasped, glad when Susie paused for breath.

'That could happen,' their dad warned. Then he told them about an orphan lamb on another farm. 'Fred Hunt said this lamb ate so much and grew so fat, he turned into a real little thug.'

'Susie won't do that!' Helen protested. Not sweet Susie.

'This lamb even attacked Fred's dog. Eventually the rascal got into the corn bin and just about ate until he burst!'

'Susie's much too gentle,' Hannah agreed with her sister. She put the bottle aside and snuggled the lamb inside the towel.

'Lambs aren't all sweet, with fleece as white as snow, you know.' David Moore didn't want them to get the idea that it would be easy.

The twins didn't believe a word; they watched Susie settle and close her eyes. Within seconds she was fast asleep.

'She won't attack you, Speckle,' Helen whispered as the dog crept up to nudge her elbow. She turned and gave him a hug. 'If it hadn't been for you, we'd never have found her!'

Speckle wagged his tail.

Susie slept and slept. David Moore got dry at last and went upstairs to work in his darkroom. Soon the twins went outside to check on the other

animals after the heavy shower. They climbed the wall into the field at the back of the house. Solo, their grey pony, came up friendly as ever. They told him about their exciting day. Then, when they got back to the house, they found Susie wide awake, snuggled up beside Speckle in his basket. Her little black face peered out from beside a surprised sheepdog.

'That's one way of keeping warm,' Hannah laughed.

Susie bleated.

'She's hungry again!' Helen cried.

They began to see why Mr Fox said he already had his hands full.

Mary Moore came home from work to find an orphan lamb in the dog's basket. 'Hello!' She put her bag down on the table with a look that said that nothing would ever surprise her.

'Isn't she sweet?' Hannah cooed.

'Isn't she gorgeous?' Helen beamed.

Their mum went to stroke the new arrival. 'She looks as if she's smiling!'

'So would you be,' their father said, 'if you were

rescued from the fell and had the twins spoiling you to death!'

Mary raised her eyebrows at him. 'She seems quite tame.' She felt the lick of the lamb's furry tongue on her palm.

'Not to mention downright cheeky, eh, Speckle?' David Moore patted the dog. The men were feeling left out.

'Dad, you like Susie, so don't pretend you don't.' Helen knew when he was kidding.

'Well, I like her too,' their mum decided. 'How long will we keep her?'

'For three months.' Hannah had listened carefully to Mr Fox's advice. 'We give her milk for the first month, and nothing else. Then we can add barley and other cereals to build up her weight, and she can go outside to graze as well.'

'Mr Fox says he'll call in to keep an eye on her,' Helen added. 'He says the main thing is to keep her warm at first.'

'Hot-water bottles!' Mary Moore said. 'We can wrap them in teatowels and they'll stay warm for most of the night. We can lay them beside her in her basket—'

'Speckle's basket,' their dad put in. 'Why not give her a knitted scarf and bobble-hat?'

'I'll give *you* a bobble hat!' she warned, going off to make some tea.

'Can we leave the stove on overnight?' Helen asked.

Their mum nodded. 'And I think there's an old duvet in the blanket chest. I picked it up in a car-boot sale. Susie could snuggle into that.'

'Stone the crows!' David Moore said, as they ran to fetch it. He'd never seen so much fuss.

'Isn't it time for her bottle?' Hannah asked, arranging the duvet into a soft cushion. Susie got up from Speckle's basket and tottered on stiff legs towards it. She sank on it with a tiny bleat and a surprised blink.

Mary came up again and slipped her arm around David's waist.

'You're all the same – you and Helen and Hannah,' he sighed. 'You can't resist a cute face.'

'Is that why we like you?' she teased.

He blushed. 'Me and Speckle on the other hand, we chaps don't fall for it, do we?'

Speckle yapped. His tail wagged.

'I'm not so sure,' Hannah laughed.

Next morning, when the twins came down before anyone else was up, they found Speckle curled up beside Susie, fast asleep on the duvet.

Three

'Susie thinks she's a dog!' Helen lay propped on her elbows in Solo's field. She chewed the end of a blade of grass and watched the lamb trying to round up the pony. Susie ran at Solo from behind, then skipped away. Speckle sat close by, watching their antics.

'Whoops!' Hannah covered her eyes as Susie fell over and tumbled down a slope. Then the lamb was up and romping towards the pony again, jumping with stiff-legged leaps. But this time Solo didn't want to play. His head went down and he snickered.

'Move on, Susie!' Helen tried out a basic

25

shepherd's command. The lamb ignored her and romped on. 'On second thoughts, she'd never make a sheepdog, would she, Speckle?' Helen rolled on to her back and stared up at the white clouds. This was their third week of looking after Susie, and the lamb had latched on firmly to the dog. They went everywhere together. Susie played follow-my-leader in the farmyard and in the field. Speckle shared Susie's warm bed and made sure she didn't come to harm.

'Go on, Speckle, see what Susie's up to.' Hannah looked round. Susie had disappeared. The dog ran to fetch her, and soon they came back together, Susie leading Speckle through the primroses at the edge of the field.

'She's a little character,' Luke Martin said whenever the twins took Susie into Doveton. Luke ran the village shop and was firm friends with the Moores. He kept white doves, played cricket in the local team, and was always keen to know what the twins were up to. He came to the doorstep to watch the lamb chasing his doves. The birds fluttered, then flew on to the roof. Susie looked up in amazement.

'Does she always try to boss people around?' he asked.

The twins nodded. 'She thinks she's a dog,' Helen explained with a grin.

'Speckle's her best friend.' Hannah saw nothing odd in this.

Luke laughed. 'I've never seen that before,' he admitted. 'A lamb and a dog!' He would tell his customers the story of the sheepdog who rescued the lamb, and how the two had become firm friends.

'Can't you keep that lamb under control?' Mr Winter complained.

Soon Susie was the talk of the village; a tame lamb from Home Farm who went about like a badly trained puppy. She dug holes in gardens and jumped over walls.

'She's only playing,' Hannah tried to explain to the ex-schoolteacher. She told Speckle to go and fetch Susie out of Mr Winter's neat front garden. Susie leapt on to the wall and bleated.

Puppy, Mr Winter's bad-tempered terrier, yapped.

'My goodness!' the strict old man admired the mighty leap. Secretly he too found Susie adorable. 'She's very agile! I expect you have to keep an eye on her?'

'Speckle does that for us,' Helen assured him. 'They're best friends.'

'Hmm.' Even Mr Winter was impressed. 'You don't come across that every day,' he admitted. 'I suppose a lamb does make a nice pet for a change, so long as she doesn't follow you to school each day. Like the nursery-rhyme, you know!' He went inside, chuckling at his little joke.

'Susie is a Herdwick lamb, one of the toughest breeds of sheep in the country,' Miss Wesley told the whole class. The teacher had taken them out on to the playing field after Hannah and Helen had spotted Susie romping on the grass with Speckle. The naughty animals had followed the twins to school!

'As you can see, Herdwick lambs have black faces.' Miss Wesley seized the chance to hold a science lesson in the sunshine. 'When she grows older, her face will turn white.'

'Please, Miss!' A hand shot up. 'What do they use their wool for?'

'For carpets, Harry, because their fleece is very tough. Susie's coat will grow long and shaggy. It won't always be pure white like this.'

'How much does she weigh, Miss?' Another eager hand punched the air.

Miss Wesley turned to Hannah. 'Can you tell us?'

'Thirty-one pounds,' she said proudly.

'How many kilos is that?' the teacher asked the class.

Meanwhile, Susie had nosed into a boy's lunchbox and was nibbling his crisps.

'She's put on a nice lot of weight,' John Fox remarked when he came up to Home Farm in late April. It was a whole month since the twins had adopted Susie. She was sturdy and strong, no longer the skinny little lamb with the feeble bleat. She charged at Speckle and butted him in the side, then she gambolled amongst the chickens in the farmyard. 'How much does she weigh, about forty pounds?'

Helen nodded. 'She's gained nearly thirty

pounds. That's good, isn't it?'

'Champion.'

Hannah and Helen smiled like proud parents.

'You can start to feed her solids. It'll help keep her digestion in order. I brought some with me in the Land Rover.' The farmer was pleased with Susie's progress. 'And now that we've got warm evenings, you can put her out to grass. Best grass, mind; the fresh growth. And make sure the pasture's clean.'

The twins took it all in.

Mr Fox glanced at them. 'You're not to get too fond of her, now. Remember, she has to come back to the flock in a few weeks' time.'

Too late. Their faces gave them away. The twins were already much too fond of Susie.

John Fox went to his Land Rover to fetch the new type of feed. Ben sat obediently in the passenger seat, tongue lolling, watching Susie and Speckle at play in the yard.

'Can he come out?' Hannah murmured. She was still shy of the gruff old farmer.

Mr Fox nodded. 'He can keep a lookout while I go in for a natter with your mum and dad.' As he

opened the door, Ben leapt down to join the game.

'Keep a lookout for what?' Helen asked.

'You need to take extra care just now.' He strode off to the house, shaking his head.

'What do you mean?' She ran after him across the yard.

'Well, now that the lamb's big enough to go out in the field, you should keep a special eye on her.'

'Oh, we won't leave her,' Helen promised. 'Anyway, Speckle will look after her.'

'Good,' he grunted.

'What's wrong?' Hannah joined them. She'd caught the edgy note in Mr Fox's voice.

He stopped in the doorway and glanced up at the fell. 'I'm not sure yet. A couple more lambs have gone missing this last week. Ben can't find them for love nor money. We've been up and down the fell a dozen times looking for them, but no luck.' Ben pricked up his ears at the sound of his name.

'How do you mean, gone missing?' Helen didn't like the sound of this. 'Have they got lost?'

'I doubt it. Lambs know to stay within sight of the mother as a rule. It's what we call a strong hefting instinct. They never wander far.'

'What then?' Hannah thought of the dangers that lambs might face on the fell.

'It could be a fox,' the farmer said, his gaze skimming the hillside. Ben, Speckle and Susie went on playing happily in the yard. 'But that's not very likely at this age. Or it could be a crow, if the lamb's sickly. They can be vicious things, crows.' Again he paused.

'Were your lambs sickly?' Hannah could tell that this wasn't the answer either. She glanced at Helen with a worried frown. Suddenly looking after Susie didn't sound so straightforward.

'No. Fit as fiddles, both of them.' He sighed.

'So, if it's not foxes or crows, what can it be?' Helen asked.

'It could be a mad dog.' This time he was deadly serious. 'But I hope not. It's bad when a dog turns on sheep. No one likes that.'

'What would you do?' Hannah felt the hairs at the back of her neck begin to prickle.

'We'd have to shoot it,' came the flat reply.

The twins swallowed hard.

'But I don't think it's that either.'

They breathed again.

'No. Like I said before, I suspect there's a sheep thief at work on the fell.'

Their eyes opened wide. This was something they'd never considered.

'That's why I'm telling you to keep an eye on Susie,' he warned. 'After all, we don't want her to be whisked off in the middle of the night, not after you've gone to so much trouble already!'

Four

'Never fear, young Susie can take care of herself,'
David Moore said when Hannah confessed her
worries. He was busy mending the farmyard gate. It
had hung off the hinge ever since the family had
arrived at Home Farm, but now the twins badly
wanted it to work. They had to keep Susie safe in
the yard. 'That lamb's a tough little so-and-so.'

Every day she grew rounder and cheekier. People
in the village would call out when they saw her
trotting down the street with the twins and
Speckle: 'Hasn't she grown!' or 'She's a little
beauty!' The kids at school petted her and fed her

tidbits. Summer had arrived. Susie was thriving.

'But another sheep went missing yesterday.' Hannah held the nails while her dad hammered at the gate. 'Mr Aysgarth at Keld House lost one of his best ewes.'

David Moore paused. 'That's bad luck on Dudley. From what I hear, he's struggling to make ends meet. He can't afford to lose his best sheep.' He hammered again and caught his thumb. 'Ouch!'

Hannah cringed. 'It always happens at night. The flocks are left up on the fell, now that the lambs are bigger. It would be easy to steal one or two when no one's around, wouldn't it?'

She spotted Helen coming up the lane on Solo. She wore a T-shirt and jeans, but even so she looked hot under her hard hat.

'Not really.' Their dad finished sucking his bruised thumb. 'For a start, all the sheep are marked with coloured dye. How would a thief get rid of that before he sold them?'

'Hmm.' Hannah frowned and flicked a fly away from her face.

'And secondly, where would he or she put them? It's one thing to kidnap a sheep, but it's another to tuck her out of sight until she's ready to be sold. Especially when all the farmers round here know the fells like the back of their hands.' He began to hammer again. 'So stop worrying. Anyway, we'll soon have this gate as good as new. Even Susie won't be able to escape!'

'Dad doesn't think there's a thief on the fell!' Hannah stood up as Helen and Solo approached. She took hold of the pony's bridle and patted his nose.

'What is it then?' Helen dismounted to lead Solo into the yard. 'What's happening to the missing sheep?'

'Maybe it's just bad luck,' their dad suggested. 'Sheep have accidents, like other animals.'

But both Helen and Hannah decided not to trust to luck. They left David Moore hard at work: *Bang-bang-bang-ouch!*, and went to brush Solo down. Susie came skipping to meet them, with Speckle trotting close behind.

'Watch out, Susie!' Helen almost tripped over her as she carried a bucket of water for Solo to drink. 'You know, whatever Dad thinks, I don't want to leave Susie out in the field overnight.'

Hannah nodded. She brushed hard at Solo's neck and shoulders. 'Anyway, she's not used to staying out. She might not like the dark.'

'And she'd miss Speckle.'

'She's so tame, she'd probably wander off with anyone who happened to pass by.'

'She could easily get lost.' Helen thought of the last good reason for them to go on spoiling and mollycoddling their pet lamb.

Susie seemed to agree. She came and played between their legs, getting in the way and leaping high into the air, as if her legs were on springs.

That night, tired out as usual, Susie came into the house, to her place by the stove. Hannah fed her milk from the bottle while Helen gave Speckle his supper. Then they both nestled in the duvet, safe and sound.

'That lamb leads the life of Riley!' John Fox grunted. He sat with his farmer friends outside Mary Moore's café in Nesfield. Saturday was market day in the small town; a time when the local farmers got together to moan about the weather, saying it was too hot or too cold, too wet or too dry. Or else they complained about the price their wool would fetch that autumn.

'She's better-fed than I am,' Fred Hunt agreed, as they stared at Susie, sitting with the twins and Speckle in the town square. Fred had run his farm at High Hartwell for thirty years, and he'd never seen a lamb so spoiled, he said.

'Those girls are much too soft with her,' Dudley Aysgarth said. He was the young man who farmed at Keld House, high on the fell; thin, with a long face and a mouth that turned down at the corners. He always wore an old grey sweater and jeans, with strong black boots, whatever the weather. 'They've turned her into a pet,' he added sourly. To him, sheep meant business, nothing more. These days business was bad, so he had reason to look glum.

John Fox sipped at the tea which Mary Moore had brought out on a tray. 'Leave them alone,' he said. 'Folk take an interest, see.' Susie was still the talk of the town. Market shoppers stopped for a chat, tourists took snapshots of the tame orphan lamb. 'It doesn't do any harm. And you know what those twins are like about animals. Daft as brushes, that's what.'

From across the square, the girls spotted the farmers. 'Let's go and say hello to Ben,' Helen suggested. The gathering crowd meant it was time to move on.

So Hannah called Speckle and Susie to heel. There were no cars allowed in the square, just people queuing for the shops and stalls. Soon they reached the pavement outside the Curlew Café.

'Thrang enough for you?' Mr Fox asked. Susie had dived straight under the table to search for cake crumbs.

The twins looked puzzled. Words round here often sounded like a foreign language.

'Thrang – busy.' He laughed. 'Anyone can tell you're not from these parts.' He winked at his friends. 'I bet you don't even know how to count!'

Helen pushed her hair back from her hot face. 'Ye-es!' She didn't realise she was being teased. 'Anyone can count.'

'Like this?' The wiry old farmer began tapping the table, one finger at a time. 'Yan, tan, tethera.'

'What?' Helen gazed from one to another.

'. . . Methera, pimp, sethera.'

'Counting sheep?' Hannah whispered. She made a good guess.

'. . . Lethera, hovera, dovera, dick!' He ran out of fingers. 'That's real counting, see!'

'Yan, tan . . .?' Hannah got the idea. This was how the old shepherds saw the sheep into the fold.

'. . . Tethera.'

'Yan, tan, tethera . . .'

'One, two, three!' Helen chimed in. It was a kind of code.

'. . . Methera, pimp, sethera,' John Fox prompted.

'Four, five, six!' the girls said.

'That's it. You should come down to Lakeside to see how it's done.' He stuffed his mouth with Mary Moore's fruitcake. 'Bring the lamb. Let her get used to the flock.'

Half-excited, half-sad, they nodded. Taking Susie to the farm would be the first step towards saying goodbye.

'You can see what farming's really about,' Fred Hunt said.

'It's about scrapie and liver-fluke and maggot-fly,' Dudley Aysgarth grumbled.

Helen curled her lip and shuddered. 'What are they?'

'Diseases,' Mr Hunt sniffed. 'Sheep get sick, you know.'

'Not if you dose them with worm-drench.' John Fox didn't like to hear so much gloomy talk.

'Aye, and dip them in the autumn.' Mr Hunt still made it sound grim. 'And I bet you two thought sheep farming was a nice, easy job!'

The twins looked upset. They didn't fancy the idea of poor Susie being dosed, drenched and dipped. It sounded horrible.

'Don't worry, it doesn't do them any harm.' John Fox laughed with a dry, wheezy sound. 'As a matter of fact, it keeps them healthy. You come down tomorrow morning and see.'

'I'll drive you down to Lakeside,' Mary Moore offered after breakfast. It was a cloudy day, but warm. The café was open on a Sunday, so she had to drive to Nesfield as usual. 'Get Susie ready. She has to get used to being an ordinary sheep sooner or later.'

'Susie will never be an ordinary sheep,' Helen

protested. 'She'll always be special.'

Out in the yard the lamb bleated to be let into the house.

'I'm sure she will be to you.' Their mum smiled at them both. 'You're going to miss her a lot when she goes back?'

They nodded.

'Never mind. She'll be up on the fell. You'll be able to visit her whenever you like.' Mary Moore had been brought up in the country. She knew what it was like to part with animals she'd grown fond of. 'Do you think Mr Fox would like some geraniums for his windowsill?' When the twins nodded, she sorted out a few nice specimens from the row of pots on a shelf. 'Ready?'

So Helen and Hannah, Speckle and Susie climbed into the battered family car and their mum drove them down the lane into the valley.

Lakeside Farm stood at the water's edge, a grey stone building with tall, round chimneys. It was so old that it was almost part of the scenery. Moss grew on the roof, the lake lapped at its feet. John Fox wasn't the sort to paint the window frames or dig a nice, neat garden. Still, he seemed pleased by

Mary's present of the bright red geraniums.

'Come on, then,' he told the twins after they'd waved their mother off. 'You two can bring these buckets of barley up the fell. And let's see if we can make a proper working dog out of that pup of yours.' He whistled to the two dogs, Ben and Speckle. They set off on the long, slow climb, with Susie trotting eagerly at their side.

'She can smell the barley,' Helen said. Halfway up the fell, other lambs in the farmer's flock spied them and came running. 'So can they!'

The lambs skipped and tumbled over the rough grass while their mothers came down more slowly, stopping every now and then to graze.

'Put the food into those trays.' Mr Fox pointed to two low metal troughs.

The twins poured until the buckets were empty. The lambs raced downhill, but Susie was there first. She began to guzzle. Meanwhile, the farmer called the dogs to heel. He chose half a dozen ewes for them to bring in and sent them off at a slow lope up the hill.

'Look at that!' Hannah watched Speckle keep tight to Ben's side. It was the first time he'd tried to herd real sheep. She held up her hands to show Helen that she had all her fingers crossed.

'Let's hope he can do it.' Helen's head went up, her shoulders back. She felt proud as she watched the two dogs round up the chosen sheep.

'Lie down!' Mr Fox shouted, loud and sharp.

The dogs crouched low to the ground.

'Come in! Away to me!'

They herded the sheep to the right, past a clump of rocks, then headed them straight down the hill.

'Lie down!' the farmer cried.

The dogs stopped. The sheep jostled and turned.

'Come by!'

Ben and Speckle moved them on, circling to keep them in a tight bunch. They brought them close to where John Fox stood.

'That'll do!' He gave a final order.

The dogs came and sat, tongues lolling, sides heaving in and out.

Helen and Hannah stood speechless with pride.

The farmer gave Speckle a quick pat. 'Not bad,' he grunted, 'for a beginner.'

Susie had finished at the food trough and came nuzzling up to Speckle.

'But don't go getting big-headed,' he warned. 'It was Ben who kept him in order. Otherwise, your young dog wouldn't have had a clue.'

Still the twins felt proud. As Mr Fox checked the blue marking on the sheep's matted fleeces, they made a fuss of clever Speckle.

'Now then.' The farmer finished dealing with the ewes and came across. 'You can leave Susie here for the day to see how she gets on.'

Helen swallowed hard. 'But—'

'We never—' Hannah held her breath.

'Thought we'd have to—'

'Leave her here today!'

He'd taken them by surprise. Susie wasn't ready to look after herself, surely.

He looked at their shocked faces. 'Don't worry, you can come and fetch her at teatime. It's not the end of the world.' He explained that from now on Susie could join the flock during the day and go home with the twins at night.

'Can we still give her a bottle when she gets back?' At last Helen found her voice.

The farmer nodded. 'Aye, for another week or so. Then she'll be weaned.'

'And she'll come here for good?' Hannah gazed up the open hillside, beyond the green valley to the wild heather and rocks.

'That's right. Your part's nearly over.' For once his voice softened. 'And a good job you've done between you.'

They gazed down at Susie frisking with Speckle; as sturdy a lamb as they could wish. But she was still young and silly. And out there was a big, wide world.

Five

'Would you mind not fiddling with your food.' David Moore watched the twins nibble at the fresh salad sandwiches he'd made for lunch.

'Sorry, Dad, I'm not hungry.' Hannah pushed her plate away and leaned her elbows on the table.

'What time is it?' Helen swung her legs and hummed.

'Ten minutes since you last asked me the same question.' He got up to answer the phone. 'What's got into you two today, as if I didn't know?'

Hannah sighed. 'How long now?'

'Three hours and thirty-five minutes.' Helen

knew that at five o'clock they could go and get Susie. Time dragged.

'Do you think she's OK?' Hannah pictured their lamb grazing on the fell.

'Yes, fine!' Helen looked on the bright side. 'Why shouldn't she be?'

'No reason.' Hannah got up and went to the window. Out in the yard, Speckle moped by the gate. He was missing Susie as well.

'I mean, she's fit and strong,' Helen pointed out.

'But she's never been out with the flock before.' Hannah couldn't help worrying. Resting her chin in her hands, she leaned on the windowsill and counted chickens. *Yan, tan, tethera.*

'Mr Fox says she'll be OK,' Helen said, trying to reassure her.

'But she doesn't have a mother to stop her wandering off like the other lambs. And you know how silly she can be sometimes.' *Methera, pimp, sethera.* The chickens clucked and pecked in the dirt.

'Not silly. More playful.' Helen rolled an apple across the table. She didn't feel as confident as she sounded.

'Whatever. She could climb up a rock and get stuck. She might fall—'

Helen jumped up. 'I'm going for a ride. Do you want to come?' Hanging around the house until teatime would drive her mad.

Hannah sighed. 'I suppose we could take Speckle with us.'

'Yes, and we could go up the fell.' Helen's face lit up.

'Great idea!' They had the same thought – they would be able to get a bird's eye view of John Fox's flock of sheep. They might even be able to spot Susie.

The twins left a note for their dad and ran to the barn. Helen grabbed Solo's tack, while Hannah unlocked the padlock on her mountain-bike and wheeled it into the yard. She would cycle beside Helen and Solo, then they would change round and Hannah would ride the pony. Speckle came running at the signs of activity. For him too it was a long day.

They were ready in record time. Helen checked the girth and mounted Solo. Hannah held the gate open, then got on to her bike to follow. It was a still, sunny day. Primroses dotted the hedge-rows as they rode by, a carpet of bluebells turned part of the hillside misty purple. Further up on the fell they could see white specks on the green background, where sheep were grazing peacefully.

Solo trotted smartly, Hannah pedalled hard, while Speckle loped along. Taking a narrow track, they followed a drover's path used by shepherds in the old days. It led them above the pastures to bare, rocky slopes. They saw the pointed rock called the Needle where they'd first found Susie, and the craggy horizon above. A clear stream ran across their path, tumbling between rocks. Solo splashed through, Speckle barked and followed. Hannah had to cross on her bike. She stood clear of the saddle and pedalled.

'Did you get wet?' Helen called from up front.

'Yep!' The water came spraying up. She was soaked.

'Me too!' They laughed and pressed on. Soon they would be able to make out the sheep more clearly. 'Down there, I can see two lambs!' Helen yelled. They leapt and scrambled up the slope. Speckle pricked up his ears and stared. 'No, it's not Susie!' Helen was disappointed. She squeezed Solo's sides and moved on.

'That's Ben, isn't it?' Helen spotted a low, dark shape streaking through the heather. The dog was rounding up a ewe and her lamb, answering John Fox's whistle. The sheep seemed to run with a slight limp. The twins waved at the farmer, who strode up the hill towards them.

'My, you're quick off the mark,' he said as he drew near. Ben hovered nearby, keeping the two sheep in check. 'It's nowhere near teatime by my watch!' He shoved his cap back and scanned the hillside.

Helen blushed. 'We were just out riding.'

'And you happened to come this way accidentally on purpose?'

'Not on purpose, exactly.' She dismounted and took off her hat. 'We haven't come for Susie, if that's what you're thinking.'

'No, of course not!' There was a twinkle in his eye as he went to check the sheep's back hoof.

'But now we're here, we might as well check

on her,' Hannah said, breathless after her hard ride.

He chuckled. 'I can read you two like a book. Go on, off you go. The lamb's down there by that clump of trees. She's right as rain, so you can stop worrying.' He picked a stone from the ewe's hoof.

They grinned. Helen led Solo. Hannah wheeled her bike and nodded at Speckle. 'Find Susie!'

The dog shot off, a bundle of black and grey speckled fur. He went like an arrow downhill, straight to the clump of trees where a single lamb nibbled grass. Susie looked up as Speckle raced towards her. She blared a greeting, leapt in the air, then came trotting to meet Speckle.

'Susie!' Hannah left her bike and began to run. The dog and lamb chased up the hill together. Speckle jumped up at Hannah in his delight. Susie bleated. 'You recognised us!' She knelt to let the lamb nuzzle her face.

'Of course she did.' Helen came up from behind with Solo. 'She wouldn't forget us in a single morning!'

John Fox could see the group fussing and

chattering. 'You've gone and done it,' he called as he came slowly downhill. 'She won't go back to grazing now she's seen you. You might as well take her with you.'

Susie's little black face smiled up at them.

'To Home Farm?' Hannah called.

'Aye. Bring her back tomorrow. We'll try again.' He trudged on, shaking his head. 'Spoiled rotten,' he grumbled. But even he couldn't keep a smile off his face as the twins, Solo and Speckle went on making much of Susie. When he reached the valley bottom with Ben, he turned to see Hannah up in the saddle with the lamb hitching a lift in front. Susie had settled, large as life, up on top, peering between Solo's ears. 'Spoiled to death,' he said again.

A week went by. The new routine worked well. Helen and Hannah would drop Susie off at Lakeside Farm on their way to school and pick her up on their way home. They missed the fun of having her in the playground, but they knew she was growing up. Her place would soon be with the flock.

'You'd never know she was an orphan,' John Fox said on the Friday morning. He stood at his farmyard gate in his shirtsleeves. 'Bold as brass, she is. Not scared of anything. You should see her climb up past High Hartwell to Keld House to find the best new grass. There's no stopping her.'

The twins enjoyed his praise. They'd done their very best for Susie, and it had paid off. She nibbled now at the farmer's empty pockets, hoping for a treat.

'We'll smit her tomorrow morning. I mean to say,

we'll give her a dab of blue dye to show where she belongs. After that, she's on her own!' He looked steadily at them, leaning on the gate.

'Won't we take her home anymore?' Hannah reached to stroke Susie's woolly head.

'No. She's a big girl now.'

'One more night,' Helen sighed.

They said a fond goodbye and promised to come and collect her after school as usual. 'Be good, Susie!' Hannah whispered. 'We'll see you later.'

Susie poked her head through the gate and bleated.

'Do you think she knows?' Hannah asked. They walked down the path towards the village. Already Mr Fox was taking Susie up the fell.

'She's probably looking forward to it,' Helen said with a sad smile. 'After all, it's where she belongs.'

Later that day, they went back to Lakeside Farm to collect Susie for the very last time. Mr Fox wasn't at home, and there was no sign of Ben in the yard.

'They must be up on the fell.' Helen was eager to go and find their lamb. She wanted a nice long evening together.

So they went to find her. Sure enough, in the distance, they saw the farmer and his dog hard at work. But Susie wasn't so easy to spot. They looked across the wild sweep of the hillside and searched behind bushes and rocks, in hollows, and along the banks of the fast-running streams. They found many lambs grazing, dozing and playing, but not Susie.

'Where can she be?' Helen paused to push her fringe back from her hot forehead. Usually Susie would spy them and come running of her own accord.

Hannah squashed a panic that was beginning to rise from a knot in her stomach. 'Let's go and ask Mr Fox.'

They ran to the edge of the pasture to tell him that Susie was nowhere to be found.

He listened, head to one side. 'Where's she at, I wonder?'

'Haven't you seen her either?' Helen cried.

'Nay, come to think of it, I haven't seen her all afternoon.'

Hannah felt the panic reach the surface. 'We've looked everywhere!' She shielded her eyes with her hand and looked again up the furthest rocky slopes.

John Fox shook his head. 'She can't just vanish.'

The twins stood deadly still, staring at one another.

'Can she? Unless—!' He scanned the hillside. 'Unless my luck's run out and that thief is back!'

Six

It was true. Susie had gone missing.

John Fox took Helen and Hannah up to High Hartwell to tell Fred Hunt. 'It's the orphan lamb. She was out with the flock for the day. When the girls came to collect her, she'd vanished into thin air!'

They sat in the old Land Rover in miserable silence.

'We searched high and low. Ben scoured the place,' he explained.

'And there was no sign?' Fred Hunt shook his head.

'I don't suppose you spotted her?' Mr Fox leaned out of his window.

'Nay, cows are my line, you know. I keep one or two sheep, but I haven't seen any lambs round this way. She must have wandered further up.'

High Hartwell wasn't the most isolated farm of the fell. There were others dotted high on the hill, sturdy stone farmhouses in the middle of nowhere.

The twins' hearts sank again. It was a huge area for them to search. And if they didn't get Susie back by nightfall, if she was lost, not stolen, then she could easily fall down a steep cliff in the dark.

'I don't know which is best,' Helen whispered. 'If a thief took her, how will we ever find her again?'

'On the other hand, if she got lost, there could be a fox or anything up there!' Hannah swallowed hard.

'Hang on, I'll ring round the other farms,' Fred Hunt suggested. He was eager to help. 'I'll try the Aysgarths at Keld House, and the Burnses at Manor Garth. I'll see if they've seen anything.' He disappeared into the house to make the phone calls, then came back out. 'Nothing,' he reported. 'No one's seen her or heard anything unusual.'

'Could we ring home, please? I'd like to tell Dad why we're late.' Crestfallen, Hannah jumped down.

'Ask him if we can stay a bit longer,' Helen insisted.

Mr Fox leant heavily on the steering-wheel and shook his head. 'You can keep on looking, but I wouldn't hold out much hope, would you, Fred?'

'Not a lot.' Mr Hunt couldn't look Helen in the eye. He dug at a clump of weeds with his toe-cap. 'It looks like a lost cause.'

Shocked and shaken as she was, Helen's jaw set in a firm line. 'We won't give up.'

'Good for you.' Fred went round to discuss events with his neighbour. 'What do you think?'

'The same as before,' came the short reply.

'A thief?'

'Aye.' He nodded, sucked his teeth and considered the possibilities.

'In broad daylight?' Fred Hunt looked about uneasily.

'It looks like it. He's got a nerve, hasn't he?'

'But where's he keeping them?'

'That's what I'd like to know.'

'I'll go down to the village and pass the word

around,' Mr Hunt promised. 'Maybe someone there has spotted something unusual.'

Hannah came out of the house as they talked. She too looked white and shocked. 'Dad says he'll come,' she told Helen. 'He'll bring Speckle and help us look.' She climbed back up into the Land Rover.

'If anyone can find Susie, Speckle can.' Helen took a deep breath. They would try again.

'Best of luck!' Fred Hunt watched them until they disappeared out of the yard.

They began anew. Speckle joined the search

party of the twins, David Moore, Mr Fox and Ben. As the sun left the fell, they retraced their steps, going higher than before. Speckle kept his nose to the ground, sniffing in vain.

The old farmer was the first to give up hope at nearly eight o'clock. 'I have to get back to the farm,' he told them. 'It's like looking for a needle in a haystack up here.'

'We'll stay,' Helen insisted. 'We could try over the other side of the fell.'

'Not tonight.' Her dad shook his head. 'There's not enough light.'

Shadows had fallen. In the silence they heard the call of birds soaring overhead and gusts of wind against the sparse trees.

'But there's another farm just over there.' Hannah pointed to a bleak square building by the side of a stream.

'That's Keld House,' John Fox said. 'The Aysgarths place.'

'Tomorrow.' David Moore stood firm. 'One lost lamb is bad enough. But if I lost you two as well in the dark, what would your mother say then?'

'Aye, come back tomorrow.' Mr Fox turned

up his jacket collar. 'That's best.'

With tears in their eyes, the twins gave up the search. They trekked down from the high slopes, still hoping against hope that they would bump into a stray lamb. There would be a faint bleat in the distance, Speckle would race to a rock, and there Susie would be, stranded on a ledge. The twins would climb and lift her to safety.

But no. They saw rabbits bolting across the slopes. Dozens, hundreds of rabbits. They saw lambs, white, speckled and black, all contentedly grazing with their mothers in the evening light. They saw a Herdwick ram with huge horns and long, shaggy fleece. He loomed out of the dusk and blared loudly.

'Come on,' their dad said at last. He stood between Helen and Hannah, one arm around each of their shoulders. 'Let's go home and tell your mum all about it.'

At Home Farm Mary Moore made them supper of hot soup and toast. Outside, the sky grew dark. There were no stars, only a thin, crescent moon. The leaves of the horse-chestnut tree by the gate flapped in the breeze. Neither Helen nor Hannah ate much. They felt empty and leaden and tired to death.

'Hannah, are you awake?' Helen lay in bed at last, staring up at the ceiling. Their early night was doing no good. She couldn't get to sleep.

'Mmm.'

'Maybe Mr Fox is right. Maybe Susie *has* been taken by a thief.'

Hannah turned on her side and held a pillow over her head. 'Don't!' She didn't want to listen. It might mean they would never see their lamb again.

'No, hang on a minute. We *have* looked in every possible place,' murmured Helen.

'Except over the far side of the fell, past Keld House.' Hannah remembered the wild, lonely ridge leading over to Manor Garth. 'Susie could have wandered that far.' She was determined to start again the next day. Even if it took all weekend, she would keep on looking until they found Susie.

Suddenly they heard a scratching noise at the door. Helen got out of bed and padded barefoot across the floor. She opened it to let Speckle creep in. 'He must have heard our voices.'

'I expect he's lonely.' Hannah sat up in bed.

Neither had the heart to send him back down to the kitchen. Instead, Hannah let him crawl under her bed for the night.

By now, Helen was wide awake. She climbed back into bed and hunched her knees towards her chest. 'If Mr Fox is right . . .'

'*If!*' Hannah insisted it was a very big if.

'Well, in a way, that would be better.' Helen had thought it through as she lay in the dark. 'You see, if there is a thief who's been stealing these sheep and lambs, that means they're probably still alive.'

'Whereas . . .'

'Whereas, if they all got lost and fell, or got caught by foxes and crows . . .' She tailed off.

'They'd be dead.' They would get trapped in a crevice and starve, or else fierce animals would hunt them down. Hannah shuddered.

'See? But if a thief's got them, he'll sell them, won't he?'

'Sooner or later,' Hannah agreed. 'And he has to keep them alive till then!'

'So all *we* have to do is find them.' It didn't sound so hard, to track down a bunch of stolen sheep and lambs. 'They can't be too far away.' Helen's mind raced on. 'What we need is clues, witnesses, anything suspicious!'

'Let's start at the beginning.' Hannah saw that this might work. 'We'll find out how many sheep have gone missing – when and where. We'll try to find a link!'

Helen sat bolt upright. 'Speckle can help!'

He came out from under the bed and rested his two front paws on her knees.

'It's Saturday tomorrow,' Hannah said. 'We'll get up early.' She reached to set the alarm.

As she eased back under the covers, Helen thought of one more thing. 'I wonder if Mr Fox has told the police?'

'About Susie being stolen?' No one had mentioned involving the police.

Helen got comfy under her duvet. 'We can find out first thing tomorrow, before we go to Lakeside.'

It felt good to make a plan; better than staying awake worrying. Still, sleep was a long time coming.

Yan, tan, tethera. Helen counted sheep. In her mind's eye she saw lambs jump over a fence. *Methera, pimp, sethera . . .* But all the lambs in her half-awake dream looked the same. They all had little black faces and cheeky smiles. They looked like Susie!

Seven

'A pet lamb?' The policeman leant over his desk and stared at the twins. He was a young constable with short fair hair and a pen tucked behind one ear. He looked as if he didn't believe a word they said.

'Not a pet exactly,' Helen explained. The tiny police station in Doveton was tucked away behind Luke Martin's shop. 'Susie belongs to Mr Fox.'

'At Lakeside?'

'Yes. But we were the ones who hand-reared her. She's twelve weeks old. Has she been reported missing?'

The policeman glanced at a computer screen, clicking at the keyboard. 'There's no missing lamb on here,' he told them. 'We've a missing handbag, two sets of keyrings, and one lost umbrella. But no lambs.'

Helen turned to Hannah. 'Maybe Mr Fox didn't get round to it yet?'

'Have you had any reports of sheep that have been stolen in the last few weeks?' Hannah asked. Surely there must be something on the police records.

'*Stolen* now, is it?' He looked again. 'One car, one bike, no stolen sheep!' He closed the file. 'You're not having me on, are you?'

They shook their heads. 'I can't understand it,' Helen said. 'A few weeks ago, Mr Aysgarth lost one of his best ewes. Why wouldn't he report it to the police?'

'Search me. But I'm telling you, he didn't.' The policeman had enough to do following up crimes that had been reported. 'Now, unless you can give me a full description of this so-called stolen lamb – height, weight et cetera, I suggest you make yourselves scarce.'

Helen stood her ground. 'Susie is a Herdwick lamb. She has a black face and legs—'

'Uh-hum!' Hannah coughed. She tried to tug Helen away from the desk. Speckle was creeping towards the door. The policeman winked and grinned.

'This is serious!' Helen whispered.

'I know, but I don't think we're getting anywhere!' Hannah kept on tugging.

'Look here.' With an effort he wiped the smile from his face. 'If this pet-lamb-that-isn't-a-pet really has been stolen, do I gather he doesn't even belong to you?'

'*She*,' Helen corrected. 'She belongs to Lakeside Farm.'

'He – she.' He shrugged. 'If she has genuinely been stolen, the proper owner must come in to report it. That's Mr Fox. Get him to do it.'

The twins nodded, wishing the floor would swallow them. From the doorstep of the station they could hear the policeman chuckling.

'It *is* serious!' Helen insisted.

'And *mysterious!*' Hannah frowned. 'You realise, none of the owners have reported anything to the

73

police!' There was nothing on the file, yet she knew sheep-stealing was a major crime.

'If it was a video or a mountain bike they'd soon report it,' Helen agreed. They walked on past Luke's shop out of the village, taking the lakeside route to Mr Fox's farm. Speckle ran ahead to greet Ben, but when they reached the gate, they saw a grim-looking farmer.

'Another one last night,' he told them. 'Before I had chance to get her marked. Gone, just like that.' He snapped his fingers.

They both gasped. 'Are you sure?'

'Yes. I was up there just after dawn, but it was too late to stop whoever it is having another go.' Sadly he shook his head.

'Mr Fox, why don't you tell the police?' Hannah was all for heading straight back to Doveton. 'We can report Susie missing at the same time.'

He narrowed his eyes, then deliberately looked away. 'Nay.'

'Why not?'

'The police can't help.' He began to trudge across the yard towards the house.

'Why not?' It was Helen's turn. She ran ahead

to attract the old man's attention.

'Because they don't know where to look, that's why.'

'But they could try.' Helen was amazed that he gave in so easily.

'Aye, and get lost on the fell,' he said. 'The police don't know their way around up there. We do. We spend all our lives on that fell, and we can't find hide nor hair of the blooming sheep!' It was obvious that he didn't think much of the townies' skill in tracking down a clever sheep thief. 'Look, let's leave them out of it. Once we bring in the police, the whole thing turns nasty. I'd rather sort it out amongst ourselves.'

And Hannah and Helen were forced to agree when the farmer pointed out that the thief, whoever it was, must be a local man. 'He must know the area as well as we do,' he confided in a low voice. 'He has to find his way about that fell, and it's often at night. Only a local could do that.'

Hannah nodded. 'I see.'

'It's probably someone who's hard up, who needs an extra bit of cash.'

'Through stealing other people's lambs!' Helen pointed out. Still, she saw that bringing in the police could upset the whole of Doveton. The police would suspect everyone and cause bad feeling in the village.

John Fox looked up at the sky. Clouds hung over the fell. He evidently needed to get on with his work. 'Those lambs are up there somewhere,' he said glumly. 'But there's not a lot we can do about it until the poor chap comes to his senses.'

Hannah chose to ignore this last remark. 'How many sheep have you lost so far?'

'Five altogether. This year's lambs. None of them were marked. Easier to sell them on, you see.'

'And what about the other farmers?'

'Let's see. I heard that three have gone from Manor Garth, and another two from Silcott Farm in the next valley.' He ticked them off on his fingers.

'And Mr Aysgarth lost his best ewe from Keld House,' Helen chipped in. 'Anyone else?'

'A couple more on Skrike Fell, beyond Silcott. They were all young 'uns.'

The twins tried hard to remember all the names,

making a plan to visit each farm in turn. 'Come on, Speckle,' Hannah said when she'd memorised the information. They had a lot to do.

'We'll go from farm to farm with Speckle,' Helen promised Mr Fox. 'We're sure to pick up a clue sooner or later.'

'Wish us luck.' Hannah stood, chin up, bracing herself for a long and tiring day.

'You'll need it,' was all he said. Ben sat at his side, quiet and subdued, watching them walk up the hill.

All the way up they kept a lookout for Susie. Speckle ran on, trying to sniff out her scent, zig-zagging from bush to rock, across streams, never stopping to rest.

'Where to first?' Helen asked. They'd reached the edge of the grazing land and looked up at the unfenced hill.

'Let's follow Speckle,' Hannah decided. Her sides ached, her throat felt raw from breathing too hard. The dog was a distant shape, scouring the slope.

'He's heading for Keld House.' Helen recognised the square farm surrounded by stone barns. It looked run-down and empty. 'We can see if Mr

Aysgarth is in, then ask him about his ewe.' She led the way across the heather, past one or two grey sheep who nibbled at tender shoots. They scuttled over loose stones and ran off as the twins went by.

'Speckle, lie down!' Hannah called as he reached the farm gate. He scratched eagerly to get inside the yard. For once, he ignored her and ran round the far side of Keld House, out of sight.

The twins broke into a run to stop him, but when they reached the gate a woman came out of the house. She stood, arms folded, watching them.

'Sorry!' Helen apologised about Speckle. 'He doesn't usually run off like that.'

The woman didn't answer. She was small and pale, with long brown hair tied back. Her face looked strained and tired. 'What do you want?'

'Mrs Aysgarth?' Helen asked. They stopped at the gate.

She nodded.

'I'm Helen Moore.'

'And I'm Hannah. We live at Home Farm.'

Still no answering smile. Mrs Aysgarth stared at them.

'We're trying to find one of Mr Fox's lost lambs,' Hannah explained. 'We heard that you'd lost a sheep a while ago?'

'My husband's not in.' She sounded blank, unfriendly. 'It's him you need to talk to.'

Hannah nodded. 'Right. We'll leave it for now. Could you tell him we came?'

The woman gave one short nod, turned and slammed the door.

Helen's eyebrows shot up. 'Phew!'

It was a setback, but it didn't put them off. On they went, calling Speckle over and over, until he came trotting out from one of the empty barns. They climbed again and soon reached the ridge where Doveton Fell gave way to Skrike Fell – another wild, steep drop into the neighbouring valley. They went from farm to farm: Manor Garth, Silcott Farm, Highgate House.

'Yes, I've lost a couple of lambs this season,' was the answer at each doorway. 'It's a complete mystery. We haven't a clue what happened to them. They vanished into thin air!'

'No, we don't want the police to be involved. That's not our way. We pass the word between ourselves. Sooner or later we'll track down the guilty party.'

'That's right, young lambs, the pick of the bunch. This thief knows his sheep. And he knows his way around.' The farmers shook their heads. One of their own kind was stealing their livelihood.

Each time, the twins looked and listened. Speckle nosed around the farmyards. But they didn't find a single clue, or any sign of Susie.

'Back to Home Farm?' Hannah suggested at last. It was mid-afternoon. They were tired and hungry.

Helen nodded. Everywhere they'd called, except at Keld House, the farmers and their wives had been kind and helpful. They'd wished them luck. 'Let's drop in on the Aysgarths on the way back,' she said. Something about the lonely farm and the unhappy woman bothered her.

So, they retraced their steps, came over the high ridge on to Doveton Fell and down the slope to the Aysgarths' farm. This time Helen made sure to keep Speckle tight at heel. He whined as he looked up at her, but he did as he was told.

They'd reached the gate and were looking across the farmyard when the door opened and Mr

Aysgarth came out. The twins took a step back; the tall man glowered at them. Under one arm he carried a shotgun.

'Go on, clear off!' His shout brought another low whine from Speckle. 'I heard you came poking your noses in earlier, letting that dog of yours run riot!'

Helen was the first to pluck up courage to speak. 'We only want to help—'

'I said, clear off.' He made as if to take the shotgun in both hands and aim. 'We don't want your help. Janet tells me you let the dog come nosing around on private property.'

'We're sorry.' Hannah saw that Dudley Aysgarth was dead set against allowing them anywhere near his farm. 'We won't let him do it again.'

He came a few steps towards them, frowning. But he let the gun drop. He seemed to calm down when he saw that they had Speckle under control. 'You can't be too careful with strange dogs, see.'

Helen took hold of Speckle's collar and whispered at him to stay. Speckle's whine had become a growl. Perhaps he understood what the gun was for.

Aysgarth stopped again and pointed. 'See!'

'Shh, Speckle!' Helen held him tight.

'He's vicious, that dog of yours!'

'He is not!' Helen rushed to defend him, but Hannah stepped in.

'It's OK, we're going.' She pulled Helen away from the gate.

'Good.' As the twins and Speckle retreated, he advanced again. 'And keep that dog well away from here,' he warned. 'This farm is private property. If I catch him here again, I won't think twice!'

Helen and Hannah began to run. They dragged Speckle with them. One glance over their shoulders told them that Aysgarth meant what he said.

He'd raised the gun above his head and shook it at them. 'Any more trouble and I'll shoot him on sight!' he yelled.

Eight

'But he can't be the thief!' Hannah protested. They raced for Lakeside Farm to tell Mr Fox what had happened. In spite of Dudley Aysgarth's scary warning, she didn't believe he was the guilty one.

'Why not?' Helen was frightened too, but there was a determined look in her eye. 'He wouldn't let us near. What has he got to hide?'

'But the thief stole one of his sheep, remember?'

'That's what *he* says!'

Hannah slowed right down. 'What? You mean he might have made it up?'

'To throw people off his scent.' Helen stood with

her hands on her hips, trying to catch her breath. They'd left Keld House far behind.

'But that's only a guess,' Hannah frowned. 'How would we prove it?' Though she didn't like Aysgarth, she wouldn't go around accusing him without proof.

'Listen, he's supposed to have lost his best ewe, right?'

Hannah nodded. 'It was weeks ago, at the start of all this.'

'But think about it. Keld House was the only farm that lost a grown-up sheep.' Helen grew more excited as she explained her theory. 'All the other farmers have lost lambs, right? That means they've been stolen before the farmers have had a chance to mark them with coloured dye!'

'What Mr Fox calls smitting them? Right – which means nobody could identify them!' Hannah got the point.

'So they'd be easy to sell at market. Except for Mr Aysgarth's ewe! But if it hasn't really been stolen, and he's the thief, that wouldn't matter would it?'

'So he's lying!'

'To put everyone off, so they won't suspect him!'

Helen was convinced she was right. 'Come on.' She set off again, forgetting in her excitement that they'd lost sight of Speckle.

'Wait!' Hannah whistled until the dog reappeared. He'd cut back towards Keld House, but came when she called. 'Speckle didn't like him either,' she reminded Helen. 'He growled at someone for the first time in his life!'

'Well, would you?' Lakeside Farm was in sight. 'If you had a gun pointing at you?'

'Where's Speckle now?' Hannah was out of breath as she gasped the question. The dog was

excited and behaving strangely.

'He's run ahead.' They followed him, shouting for Mr Fox to come and listen to their brilliant solution.

'Nay.' Mr Fox shook his head. 'Not Dudley Aysgarth.' He'd invited them into his kitchen. It was dark and old-fashioned, lined with shelves that were stacked with plates and cups.

'Why not?' Helen thought she'd explained clearly. 'Why else would he want to keep us out?'

'You don't think he'd hide stolen lambs in his barn, do you?' He sat them down and made them catch their breaths.

'He could do.'

'Nay, he can't keep them indoors. They need good fresh grass, out in the open. This thief has got them out on the fells somewhere, believe me.'

For a moment, Helen faltered.

'Anyhow, Dudley's family has been at Keld House for as long as I can remember,' Mr Fox went on. 'His father had it before him, and his grandfather before that. The Aysgarths are well known round here. They're poor all right. In fact, they only just scrape a living, some of those hill farmers. But no one's ever accused them of being dishonest.' He went on shaking his head, but the twins noticed that he refused to look them in the eye.

'Then why was Speckle so interested in Keld House?' Hannah asked. She backed Helen's theory, but saw they would have a tough time convincing him. 'Why did he go running off round the back of the farm?'

'Don't ask me.' With a shrug the old farmer went to the doorway. 'But suppose you're right? Suppose it's Dudley who's stealing the lambs? I'm not saying it is him, mind. I'm saying just suppose. Right, he's got a bunch of them hidden on the fells. He'll hang on until September, then he'll put them in his trailer and drive them to market in Kendal, hoping no one will recognise them.'

'And will you let him get away with it?' Helen jumped up from her seat at the table. 'Will you just let him cart Susie off and sell her to any-old-body?'

'Shh!' He raised his hand to show he hadn't finished. 'What will he make out of it? A few extra pounds to help him through the winter if he's lucky.' John Fox turned to face the twins. 'Just think how bad it must be for him and his wife if he has to resort to stealing a few sheep.'

Helen and Hannah were struck by the serious look on his face.

'What would happen if you two were right and we turned him over to the police?'

They shook their heads.

'I'll tell you. They'd take him to court. His name would be ruined up and down these fells as far as Nesfield,' he said sternly. 'He could even go to prison. Then what? His wife would have to sell the farm. That would be it – no more Aysgarths at Keld House.'

'But—' Hannah began one last protest on Susie's behalf.

Again he raised his hand and shook his head. 'Nay,' he sighed.

Helen thought it through. 'Will you just let him go on stealing your lambs?' she asked quietly. She wondered whether he'd suspected Aysgarth all along.

He turned away, patted Speckle and called Ben in from the yard. 'He'll stop now, you'll see. There'll be no more lambs going missing on Doveton and Skrike, not now he knows you've cottoned on.'

They understood that it would be much too risky for Aysgarth to go on stealing sheep.

'Dudley's no fool. He'll hang on to the ones he's got, but he won't do it again.'

'And what about Susie?' This was Hannah's one and only thought.

Mr Fox lifted his cap from the hook on the door. He pulled it well down over his forehead and gave them a final piece of advice. 'Forget about Susie. Leave the Aysgarths alone. In fact, forget the whole business!'

Easier said than done. The twins and Speckle trudged back to Home Farm. Even Solo couldn't cheer them up. They sat on the wall overlooking his field and watched him come cantering up.

'Never mind, Solo, we'll take you out tomorrow,' Helen promised. 'But not tonight.' Neither of them had the heart to saddle him up and go on their usual Sunday evening ride.

Instead, they did jobs around Home Farm. They fed lettuce to the rabbits in their hutch, they scattered corn for the hens and grain for Lucy the goose. Then they laid the table for tea before their mum got back from work, and helped their dad bake a flan and some scones.

'Forget about her, eh?' David Moore dusted flour on to the baking-board.

'That's what Mr Fox told us to do.' A tear trickled down Hannah's cheek. She felt her bottom lip tremble.

Helen thumped the raw pastry on to the board. 'How are we supposed to do that? Susie's hidden away on the fell, and Mr Aysgarth knows where she is! How can we forget her?'

'I know it's hard,' he admitted. 'But John Fox is right in a way. I feel sorry for the Aysgarths if stealing their neighbours' sheep is the only way they can make ends meet.'

Mary Moore thought so too, when she came in and heard their story. 'Firstly, you've no proof that Mr Aysgarth is guilty,' she reminded them. 'Secondly, Susie belongs to Mr Fox. And if he doesn't want to take things further, I'm afraid there's nothing you can do.'

'Look at it this way,' their dad said, 'you did your very best.' He stood at their bedroom door, waiting for them to settle down for the night.

'You just have to let it rest, OK?'

He switched off the light and they listened to his footsteps going downstairs.

'Our best wasn't good enough!' Helen whispered across the dark room.

'Poor Susie!' Her proper place was on Doveton Fell, not squashed into a dark trailer, being driven to Kendal market. 'Helen?'

'What?'

Hannah's voice drifted through the dark. 'Can we find our way to Keld House in the dark?'

There was a long silence. 'I think we can. If we take Speckle with us. When?'

'Tonight.' Hannah heard Helen take a deep breath to steady herself. 'After Mum and Dad have gone to bed.'

It would be risky. Even the farmers who'd lived here all their lives didn't like to go on the fell after dark. 'OK,' Helen whispered.

They waited. Minutes seemed like hours. At half-past ten they heard footsteps on the stairs. By eleven o'clock the house was quiet. At midnight, when they were certain they could get out without being heard, they crept downstairs in their jeans and sweaters. Once they reached the kitchen, they put on their jackets and trainers.

'Shh, Speckle!' Helen hissed. He jumped up and gave a little yelp. 'You're coming too!'

Outside in the farmyard, the moon had risen high above the chestnut tree. Silvery clouds scudded across its face, eerie and beautiful. Hannah zipped her jacket. 'Ready?'

'Let's go.'

Together, with Speckle tucked in behind them, they ran silently across the yard into the lane.

Nine

'Thank goodness there's a moon.' Helen looked up at the sky. 'Otherwise we wouldn't be able to see a thing.'

Doveton Fell seemed vast and empty. They'd climbed higher than Keld House, close to the Needle. From there they would creep down to the farm from behind and send Speckle into the barns to hunt for clues.

'It's not bad once your eyes get used to the dark.' It was true they'd slipped and stumbled across some of the shadowy hollows, but the moon gave enough light to follow tracks through the heather up on to the scree slope. Sure-footed as ever, Speckle had guided them.

Hannah and Helen were glad they'd brought him along. When something scuttled through the bushes, or a black shape flapped and squawked out of the heather, they knew the dog would look after them. When they lost the track, Speckle would find it again.

'Good boy, Speckle.' Helen peered in the direction of Keld House. She could just make out a square outline and a straggle of barns. 'Let's find Susie!' She let go of his collar and sent him on, watching him streak away down the hill.

They ran after him for all they were worth. 'He's picked up a trail.' Hannah saw the white flash of his tail far ahead. 'He has! Look, he's found something!'

In the distance Speckle gave a high, sharp bark. Then he plunged on into the darkness.

'Where is he? Can you see him?' Helen slowed down and steadied herself by clinging on to a low branch. Keld House lay a couple of hundred metres below.

'He must have charged ahead, following Susie's trail!' Hannah's heart gave a lurch. They couldn't call or whistle in case they woke the Aysgarths. 'Come on, we'd better find him quick!'

They ran to the farm, which stood quiet in the moonlight – no sound, no lights, no sign of life. The twins didn't even dare to whisper as they climbed the stone wall into the farmyard and crept towards the first barn. Helen pointed to a half-open door and went towards it. There was enough room to slide through without disturbing it on its rusty hinges. But inside there was dense blackness and silence.

'Speckle!' Hannah's whispered call hissed and echoed.

'No.' Helen shook her head and began to back out of the barn. 'He's not here.'

Suddenly the door hinges creaked. The twins spun round. There was silence again.

'It was the wind,' Helen said. But her skin prickled with fear. For a moment she'd imagined someone outside the door. 'Let's get out of here!' In her fright she stumbled against a hollow metal can. It clashed and rolled across the stone floor.

Hannah gasped. They both dashed for the door, not caring now if the hinges creaked. They flung it open and began to run across the yard. A light went on in the house, then another. Before they reached the wall, the front door crashed wide open. A tall figure let his dog off the leash with a harsh command. It leapt from the doorway and cannoned towards them, snapping and barking. The twins cowered, as Mr Aysgarth stepped out and pointed a torch. It caught them red-handed in its beam of bright light.

'It could have been a gun.' Half an hour later Mr Aysgarth handed the twins over to Mary Moore, who'd driven up to Keld House to collect them. The dog, Shep, still growled on the end of his chain. 'Luckily it was only the torch I was pointing at them!'

'I'm very sorry, Mr Aysgarth.' Mary's face was tense, her voice strained. 'I don't know what got into them. But I promise it won't happen again.'

'Creeping about in the dead of night; what was I supposed to think?' He glowered as the twins got into the car. 'It could have been burglars, or this sheep stealer we've got prowling about! Like I say, they're lucky I didn't take a pot shot at them instead of letting Shep loose.'

She nodded. 'Don't worry, I'll deal with it.'

'I don't want them causing any more trouble.'

Miserably Helen and Hannah sat hunched in the car while their mum tried to put things right with the angry farmer. His wife, Janet, stood at the door without saying a word. At last it was over and they backed out of the farmyard on to the track away from Keld House.

'What about Speckle?' Helen asked in a husky whisper. She felt choked; ashamed of the fright they must have given their mum and dad when the phone rang and they'd learnt what had happened.

'Speckle can look after himself.' Mary Moore looked straight ahead. Her hands gripped the steering-wheel.

Hannah suffered in silence. What if Mr Aysgarth went and found him in another barn? He would send Shep in to fight him. Shep was big and strong, trained to attack strangers.

Their mother drove them home without saying another word. But as their dad stood waiting at the door and they got out of the car, she took them each by the hand. 'We're glad you're safe and there's no harm done,' she said. 'We even see why you thought you had to do this. Susie was very important to you, we know that.'

'But – ' David Moore took over and led them inside – 'we never want you to do anything like this ever again. No excuses, we just want you to promise!'

Eyes glistening, they nodded.

'Good. Well, get to bed. In the morning your mum and I will decide what to do next.'

Hannah fought back the guilty tears. 'Dad, did Speckle come home?'

He frowned and shook his head. His silence meant, 'You see what trouble you've caused by being so foolish? Not only is Susie lost, but now Speckle's gone missing as well.'

'We'll look tomorrow,' their mum said wearily.

It was the worst night of their lives as they stumbled upstairs. They got into bed without saying anything, pulled the covers over their heads and counted the minutes until daylight.

* * *

'You must not go near Keld House!' David Moore spelt it out for them. Speckle hadn't come home during the night and he'd decided that the twins could go on the fell to look for him after school. 'And call in at home first. I'll be asking around meanwhile. John Fox might hear something, or Fred Hunt. We'll have to keep our fingers crossed.'

All day Helen and Hannah lived in a nightmare from which they couldn't wake up. Too upset even to talk about what had happened, they went to lessons imagining what might have happened to poor Speckle. There was fierce Shep for a start. And then there was the terrible memory of Dudley Aysgarth standing with his gun raised above his head the first time they had seen him; his warning that next time he would shoot Speckle on sight.

In the playground after school, Miss Wesley noticed that they weren't themselves. She stopped to ask if she could help.

'We've lost Speckle,' Helen confessed.

'Oh, I'm sure he'll find his way home eventually,' she said gently. 'Sheepdogs are very clever. Why don't you go and see?'

It was a long walk through the village and up their lane to Home Farm. But there was no Speckle waiting at the gate to welcome them; only their dad shaking his head. 'No news,' he said quietly. 'I've got everyone keeping a lookout though.'

The nightmare went on. The twins left their schoolbags and went out on to the fell. It was a windy, cloudy afternoon of sudden gusts and short, sharp showers.

'Remember what we said,' David Moore called. He was gentle but firm. 'Concentrate on looking for Speckle and don't go near Keld House. Come back by six o'clock, no later.'

They agreed. At least they were out looking at last.

'We have to think!' Helen said. They'd decided to take their bikes, to cover more ground. It was tough going along the drovers' tracks, especially when the wind was against them. 'To start with, where did we last see Speckle?'

'By the Needle.' Hannah remembered exactly; the last flash of Speckle's white tail as he raced across the dark moor.

'Right. But he didn't go to Keld House as we thought.' Without putting it into words, they both decided to change direction and head for the pointed rock. They would start from there. 'If he had, he would have come to help when we were in trouble.'

'So he headed somewhere else in the dark. But where?' Hannah racked her brains. 'Surely if he picked up Susie's scent, he would have traced it to Keld House?'

'Unless we were wrong about Mr Aysgarth?' For a moment Helen wavered.

Hannah ignored her. 'No, wait a minute! Remember what Mr Fox said? He said the thief wouldn't keep the lambs in a barn, but out in the open!'

'That's right, on good grazing land to fatten them up.' Helen braked and eased her bike around a boulder on the track.

'Land that no one knows about, somewhere cut off, but somewhere that has plenty of grass. Like a secret fold!'

Helen nodded. 'Down a hidden track, at the end of a steep gulley.' Could there be such a place on Doveton Fell?

'And that's where Speckle must have followed the trail to!' That was it; he must have circled around Keld House and kept going. 'If only we'd been able to keep up,' she sighed.

For the first time since Dudley Aysgarth had trapped them in his torchbeam, their spirits revived. That must be it; the lambs were penned in secret. The thief was letting them feed, waiting for autumn when he would take them off to market. Clever Speckle had tracked them down, and now he himself was being kept prisoner!

'OK, if Speckle circled round the farm and carried on, that's what we have to do now.' Helen spotted a track they could take along the ridge.

Hannah remembered their dad's order to steer clear of Keld Farm. 'Let's ride on the Skrike Fell side of the ridge so the Aysgarths don't see us.'

Helen agreed, though it was extra work to cycle over the top. They dropped down until they came within sight of Manor Garth and Silcott Farm, then they cut back up to the top. Eventually, when they'd made a wide detour, they reappeared on top of the ridge, looking down on Doveton once more.

'Where to now?' Hannah scanned the valley. Way below, the low walls made a patchwork of green fields. Further up the slope there were rough ferns and heather, then the bare stone where they now stood. 'Where could a thief hide a dozen lambs and a dog?'

Helen studied the hillside. It had to be somewhere with trees perhaps, or a stream that cut into the rock and made a deep gulley. Yes, there was a stream a bit further along the ridge, bubbling up from a spring and splashing down the slope. After a while the water disappeared amongst rocks and trees. 'Let's try that!'

They rode over the loose stones, hair flying back in the wind. When they came to the stream they left their bikes and climbed down on foot. The water cut steeply into the rock. It gushed and splashed towards the trees, growing steeper still. The twins scrambled down, feeling the air turn damp and cold as they entered the gulley.

'How could he get sheep into and out of here?' Hannah gasped. She looked up at the towering wet rocks.

'There must be another way in. This end is a dead-end. Even sheep couldn't climb up here. It's turned into a sort of waterfall, look!'

Now the stream splashed white and foaming over a ledge of rock. They picked their way wide of the fall. Wet ferns tripped them, trees clung to bare rock, their roots twisting underfoot. Then suddenly the narrow gulley widened out. The sheer rock opened out onto a flat ledge, which they headed for. They made it to level ground, close to the rushing water, catching their breath, hardly daring to look around.

But then, above the crashing roar of the waterfall, they heard something else. A new sound, sharp and high. There across the green clearing was an animal tethered to a wooden stake. It strained at a thick rope, yelping at them.

'Speckle!' Hannah and Helen rushed to the spot. They sank to their knees and threw themselves around his neck. Speckle licked them and barked with joy. He yelped to be free of the rope.

Hannah caught hold of it. The knot was cruelly tight and impossible to untie.

'Wait!' Helen ran to the stake and pulled. It was hammered deep into the solid ground. 'We'll get you free,' she promised Speckle. 'Come on, Hannah, help over here!'

They heaved and pulled. 'Lie down, there's a good dog,' Hannah cried. To have him straining at the rope made freeing him more difficult. She seized a sharp stone nearby and began to dig at the earth to dislodge the wooden stake.

Helen worked with her. 'Where are the lambs?' The small clearing was empty except for Speckle, but she felt they were close to discovering where the thief kept the stolen sheep.

'Once we get Speckle free, he'll show us.' Hannah kept on digging. At last the stake came loose. They stood up and heaved until they uprooted it from the earth.

Speckle felt the rope go slack. He jumped up and ran, dragging the rope and wooden pole. It bumped over the rough grass. Then he came to a ledge, paused; then bounded clean out of sight.

'Quick!' Helen scrambled after him.

They ran to the edge of the cliff. There was a sheer drop into a second clearing surrounded by trees. There, quietly eating the grass, as if nothing in the world was amiss, were a dozen healthy, stolen lambs.

Ten

'Susie!' Hannah pointed to the far edge of the little flock. Speckle was down there too, trailing his rope. A lamb with a black face and legs stared up at him as he bounced across. She bleated and trotted to meet him. The two friends were together again.

Helen and Hannah looked at each other and laughed. Speckle and Susie were safe. Now all they had to do was to get them out of here. They stared down at the sheer drop; it was twice as tall as they were. The landing was loose stones. But there was nothing else for it.

They stood at the edge. The wind blew against

them, carrying big, cold drops of rain. Susie and Speckle came trotting back across the secret fold, bleating and barking up at them. Hannah closed her eyes and took a deep breath. Helen looked once more at their stony landing. Then they jumped out into mid-air.

Helen landed and rolled, relaxing as she hit the ground. Hannah managed to stay on her feet. She pulled Helen up and they ran to throw their arms around Susie this time. In the middle of this new clearing, they knelt down and hugged her.

All the other lambs who had scattered as first the dog and then the two girls had jumped down into their private pasture, grew braver and trotted near. Rain had begun to fall heavily, and wind drove down the gulley, but Helen and Hannah hardly noticed.

'You'd never guess it was here.' Hannah was the first to look around. The clearing was hidden from above by the spreading branches of the trees, and the only way out seemed to be at the other end of the clearing, through a gap between the gnarled trunks. The gap was barred by a strong wooden gate. The twins peered at it through the rain, wondering how they could drive the lambs from the fold.

'It's the perfect hiding place,' Helen agreed. Beyond the gate there had to be a path leading to another drovers' track perhaps. For a moment she thought she caught a new sound, paused and stopped to listen, then shook her head.

'What?' Hannah strained to hear.

'Nothing. I thought I heard a noise, but it's gone now.'

'What sort of noise?' Hannah could only hear the rain lashing the trees and the rocks, the splash and tumble of the stream behind them.

Helen listened again. Her eyes grew startled. 'Can you hear it? An engine, coming this way!' She ran to the gate that kept the stolen lambs locked in the fold.

'Yes!' It rumbled nearer, but still invisible. 'It's a car!'

'Bigger than that. A truck or a trailer!' Helen's wet, cold fingers struggled with the chain that fastened the gate. Someone was coming. Now, when they were on the point of rescuing Susie, they were trapped again.

'Is there another way out?' Hannah turned desperately to look. Speckle jumped up at the gate, scratching to be free before it was too late. All the lambs gathered round and jostled. It was no good; they were in a dead-end. Steep rocks rose to either side, and the waterfall blocked the far side.

An engine roared nearer, there was a crunch of heavy wheels over loose stones. A Land Rover loomed through the grey rain, chugging uphill towards the gate, headlights full on, bumping and pulling a trailer in its wake.

'Hide!' Helen let the chain drop. She looked for somewhere out of sight, then saw a rock big enough for them all to crouch behind. 'Come by, Speckle!' Helen hissed, pulling Hannah with her.

The dog settled close at Susie's heels, creeping at her, herding her towards the rock.

'That's it, come by. Good boy!' Just in time, Helen reached out and grabbed hold of Susie. They reached the safety of the rock and dived behind it, without daring to look.

The Land Rover stopped at the gate. The driver kept the engine running. A door slammed, a chain rattled, the gate swung open. The thief had arrived.

From behind the rock Helen and Hannah heard the lambs bleat. A dog barked. Helen held her finger to her lips to stop Speckle from answering back. After a while, the bleating died down, and there was the sound of hard hoofs trampling up a metal ramp, then more bleats; a loud, frightened chorus.

'He's taking them away!' Helen whispered. Rain streamed through her hair, down her face.

'He'll count them before he goes!'

'He'll find there's one missing!'

'He'll come to look!'

Any second now, they expected to see the tall, lean figure of Dudley Aysgarth leaning over them, his dog at his side. They crouched closer against the rock, praying that Speckle wouldn't bark, or Susie break loose.

A dog did come, drenched to the skin, sniffing and poking through the bushes. A voice called after him. 'That'll do!' Footsteps followed, closer and closer.

Hannah and Helen got to their feet. They might as well confront Aysgarth, let him do his worst. Stepping out from behind the rock, they came face to face with the thief.

The figure stopped in its tracks. It was shorter than Aysgarth, slighter, with a hood pulled low over its face. The twins stared at a small woman in a heavy blue jacket.

'Mrs Aysgarth!' They'd been wrong all along. It was the wife from Keld House, the woman who never said a word.

Janet Aysgarth couldn't deny it. She'd been even more shocked than the twins when they'd stood up from behind the rock. She'd stepped back and slumped against a tree. 'Dudley doesn't know,' she said, before they had time to say a word. 'I wanted to help. It was the only way I could think of!'

She knew the game was up. She'd gone and let the lambs out of the trailer and herded them back into the fold. 'Here's all the evidence you need,' she'd said bitterly.

The evidence stared John Fox, Fred Hunt and her husband in the face when Hannah and Helen brought them up to the secret fold. 'She was trying to get rid of them before we got on to her,' John Fox explained. 'She thought she could drive them over to Kendal without Dudley getting to know, since she realised you two were on Susie's trail. She came over last night to catch Speckle and tie him up, then she waited until her husband had his back turned and drove here with the trailer. She would just about have got away with it if it hadn't been for you.'

Helen and Hannah watched Dudley Aysgarth as he helped Fred Hunt to separate the lambs, ready to take them back to their owners. Poor Janet Aysgarth had driven from the clearing, straight home to confess to her husband. He'd rung John Fox and told him the truth.

'Will Mrs Aysgarth get into trouble?' Hannah asked.

'No, we've decided not to press charges,' the old farmer told them. 'We've got our lambs back, thanks to you. What would be the point?'

They were glad to agree. The Aysgarths had had enough of a shock for one day.

Only one thing bothered Hannah. 'Did the Aysgarths really lose their best ewe?' She watched the men herd the lambs into Land Rovers parked on the secret track.

Mr Fox nodded. 'That was genuine. It's a mystery

we'll never solve, I suppose.'

As the clearing emptied, the twins went slowly towards Dudley Aysgarth, with Susie and Speckle following. Hannah spoke for them both. 'We hope everything will work out OK,' she said quietly.

Mr Aysgarth gave a faint nod. 'Thanks.' Then he stopped, half-in and half-out of the Land Rover. 'It's been a hard year for us,' he told them. 'All work and no play, and still we couldn't manage. Janet only did it to get us out of a hole.'

'We know.' Helen was glad the police wouldn't be involved.

'We'll try and give you a better welcome next time you call in at Keld House,' he said, climbing up behind the wheel. 'That is, if you care to call?'

'Yes,' they said. 'We'll come and visit.'

'Janet would like that,' he said with a smile.

'Come on, get in.' John Fox told the twins to bring Susie and Speckle. Theirs was the last Land Rover to leave the scene. They reversed one at a time down the track out on to the drovers' road. 'Your mum and dad will be waiting to know that you're safe.'

They met up with them at Lakeside Farm. Mary

and David Moore had received a phone message saying that all was well; the twins had found Susie and Speckle. No one was hurt and the sheep stealer had been caught.

'Heroes, eh?' Their dad grinned. He held out his arms to hug them both.

'Thank heavens!' Their mum had tears in her eyes.

'Speckle's the real hero,' Hannah insisted.

'You all are.' John Fox stood by, a smile creasing his face from ear to ear. 'Now let's get this lamb out to graze.'

Susie pranced, skipped and jumped, until Speckle and Ben came to sort her out.

'Come in!' the farmer called.

They all watched the dogs herd the lamb into the field.

'Away to me!'

Susie ran up the slope, chased by the dogs in a friendly race towards the rest of the flock.

'Come by, Ben! Come by, Speckle!' Mr Fox steered them off to the left. 'Right, that'll do!'

The two sheepdogs came to a halt and sat quite still. Susie ran on. Soon she was a tiny white speck

on the hill.

'Everybody happy? David Moore asked.

The twins gazed after Susie. A weak, watery sun had appeared on the horizon. Their lamb stopped to graze. Speckle turned and loped towards them. They turned to their mum and dad and nodded. It was as if orphan Susie had never been lost. She was home on the hillside where she belonged.

h HODDER

Another Hodder Children's book

If you've enjoyed this book, look out for the other books in the Home Farm Twins series.

SPECKLE THE STRAY

Jenny Oldfield

A lost puppy, trapped in a dangerous quarry! Has he been abandoned there?

The twins long to keep him – but what if the owner comes back?

If you've enjoyed this book, look out for the other books in the Home Farm Twins series.

SINBAD THE RUNAWAY

Jenny Oldfield

Sinbad needs a home while his owner is on holiday.

The twins adore the fluffy black cat, but he leaves a trail of chaos wherever he goes!

And then he runs away.

Can Helen and Hannah find him – before he gets into real trouble?

If you've enjoyed this book, look out for the other books in the Home Farm Twins series.

SOLO THE HOMELESS

Jenny Oldfield

Solo's owner doesn't want him any more.

Helen and Hannah would love to have the pony – but their parents can't possibly afford to buy him.

Can Speckle, the twins' lovable dog, solve the problem?

Home Farm Twins
JENNY OLDFIELD

❏	661275	Speckle The Stray	£3.50
❏	661283	Sinbad The Runaway	£3.50
❏	661291	Solo The Homeless	£3.50

All Hodder Children's books are available at your local bookshop or newsagent, or can be ordered direct from the publisher. Just tick the titles you want and fill in the form below. Prices and availability subject to change without notice.

Hodder Children's Books, Cash Sales Department, Bookpoint, 39 Milton Park, Abingdon, OXON, OX14 4TD, UK. If you have a credit card you may order by telephone – (01235) 831700.

Please enclose a cheque or postal order made payable to Bookpoint Ltd to the value of the cover price and allow the following for postage and packing:
UK & BFPO – £1.00 for the first book, 50p for the second book, and 30p for each additional book ordered up to a maximum charge of £3.00.
OVERSEAS & EIRE – £2.00 for the first book, £1.00 for the second book, and 50p for each additional book.

Name ....

Address ....

....

....

If you would prefer to pay by credit card, please complete:
Please debit my Visa/Access/Diner's Card/American Express (delete as applicable) card no:

Signature ....

ExpiryDate ....